# TY'S TRIPLE TROUBLE

by Eleanor May

illustrated by Amy Wummer

Kane Press, Inc.
New York

**For Raven, Jasmyne, Dylan, and Macie—E.M.**

**NOTE:** All the stories in the sidebars are about real kids!

Text copyright © 2007 by Eleanor May
Illustrations copyright © 2007 by Amy Wummer

Library of Congress Cataloging-in-Publication Data

May, Eleanor.
   Ty's triple trouble / by Eleanor May ; illustrated by Amy Wummer.
      p. cm. — (Social studies connects)
   Summary: Ty takes on too many volunteer projects, with near-disastrous results.
   ISBN-13: 978-1-57565-237-5 (alk. paper)
   ISBN-10: 1-57565-237-4 (alk. paper)
      [1. Voluntarism—Fiction.]   I. Wummer, Amy, ill.  II. Title.
   PZ7.M4513Ty 2007
   [E]—dc22
                                                       2006026408

10 9 8 7 6 5 4 3 2 1

First published in the United States of America in 2007 by Kane Press, Inc.
Printed in Hong Kong.

Social Studies Connects is a registered trademark of Kane Press, Inc.

Book Design: Edward Miller

www.kanepress.com

Skateboarders do not wear aprons.

Helmets? Yes. Knee pads? Sure. Awesome sneakers? Absolutely. But aprons? No way!

"I can't go skateboarding, Ty," Nate tells me. "Gram's helping me bake cookies for the senior center. It's my volunteer project."

Oh, no! The project!

Everybody in our class has to do a volunteer project, but I just can't come up with an idea.

"What are you going to do?" Nate asks.

"Haven't thought of anything yet," I tell him.

"Better start thinking," he says. "The report is due on Tuesday."

Tuesday! Then I only have three days left!

A **volunteer** is someone who offers to do work for free. If you have ever offered to do a job for no pay—like taking care of a class pet, or helping a neighbor with some yard work—you have **volunteered**.

I follow Nate into the kitchen. "Those cookies sure smell good. Maybe I could help you bake."

Nate gives me a look. "Ty, you can't even make a peanut butter sandwich."

"I can be the taste tester," I say. "See if the cookies are good enough to sell."

"Thanks, but no thanks," he says.

I go to Kelly's house. "Want to practice ollies in the park?" I ask. An ollie is a skateboard jump.

She shakes her head. "I'm taking Princess to the hospital."

I look at Princess. She seems fine, unless you count the drool. "What's wrong with her?"

"Nothing," Kelly says. "It's my volunteer project. We're going to visit sick children."

"They let dogs in people hospitals?" I ask.

"Princess has special training," Kelly says. "She took a test to prove she's a Canine Good Citizen."

"Did she bark the Pledge of Allegiance?"

Kelly laughs. "Of course not. She had to show that she can sit, stay, come when called, and be polite around strangers and other dogs."

Boy, I wish my teacher gave tests like that!

**Not Just for Grownups**
Kids who volunteer make a difference! Lots of volunteer groups—like Habitat for Humanity—have special projects that kids can do.

I go to the park, but it's no fun practicing ollies all alone—especially since I'm not having much luck.

The older kids make ollies look so easy. Pop down. Snap up. Soar! How do they do it? They must glue their skateboards to their feet!

One girl is doing all kinds of terrific tricks, like caspers and kickflips. Hey—it's Anita, the new girl at school. She's not an older kid. She's in fourth grade, like me. Wow, she is *so* cool.

I try another ollie—and flub it. Now I feel even worse. So I head for home.

I still have to come up with a volunteer project. But what?

I could bake cookies, like Nate. But my grandma is more into tofu than cookies.

I could take my guppy, Skip, to the hospital—but he's kind of boring.

My neighbor, Mr. Soo, is sitting on his porch.

"Hey, Ty," he says. "What did the pig say to the horse?"

I'm not in the mood for riddles, but I like Mr. Soo, so I play along. "What?"

"Why the long face?" He laughs at his own joke.

I tell Mr. Soo about the project. "What can I do? I don't know how to do anything special."

"Maybe you could learn a skill," he says, "like sign language."

Hmm. I imagine trading secret messages with Kelly and Nate in science class. Awesome!

"Can I learn sign language by Tuesday?" I ask.

He smiles. "It may take a bit longer than that."

Mr. Soo tells me I can use skills I already have, like reading and writing. "When I first came to this country," he says, "a volunteer helped me fill out forms so I could find a job. Now I help tutor other immigrants."

He shows me a photo. "This is Mr. Gupta. I'm teaching him English."

**Help Others—Help Yourself!**
Volunteering isn't just good for others. It can be good for you, too! It's a great way to meet people and make friends who have the same interests as you.

When I get home, my mom is in the kitchen with her friend Mrs. Mallory.

"I don't know what to do. Mimi's having such a hard time with math," says Mrs. Mallory. Her daughter Mimi is two years younger than I am.

I think of what Mr. Soo told me about using skills I already have. Math is something I'm pretty good at—especially second-grade math!

"I could tutor Mimi," I pipe up.

Mrs. Mallory is so happy, she offers to pay me.
"No, thank you," I tell her. "I'm volunteering."
My mom is proud. Mrs. Mallory is glad that
Mimi will get help. And I've solved the problem
of what to do for my project. Everybody wins!

**Personality Quiz!**
Volunteering can be fun, especially
if you do things you enjoy. Do you
like reading? Volunteer to read with
younger kids at your library or school.
Do you like animals? Ask a local
animal shelter how you can help out!

The next morning, I'm waiting for Mimi when the phone rings. It's Nate.

"Gram and I both have colds!" he says. "Can you take our cookies to the bake sale? It can be your volunteer project."

I already have a project, but I don't want to disappoint Nate. "I'll be right over," I tell him.

The doorbell rings.

Uh-oh! I forgot about Mimi.

"Why don't you come with me to the senior center?" I suggest. "I can help you with your math after we drop off the cookies."

"Sure," Mimi says cheerfully. "Math can wait!"

"Hey, Ty!" Mr. Soo calls me over. "Here's a volunteer project! I have to go out, and I don't want to leave Puff alone. Can you cat-sit for me?"

He looks so hopeful, I just can't say no.

Now I have three projects. How can I tutor Mimi, cat-sit Puff, and take Nate's cookies to the senior center—all at the same time?

I know! I'll ask Nate to watch Puff while Mimi and I go to the center. Simple.

Or maybe not so simple.

*"Ah-ah-CHOO!* You can't leave that cat with me." Nate sniffles. "I'm allergic!"

"How about if Mimi stays here?" I say. "You can help her with her math."

"Yuck!" Mimi makes a face. "He's all germy!"

"I think I'm allergic to second-graders, too," says Nate.

Outside the senior center, Mimi asks, "Do they let kitties inside?"

"Sure. They even let dogs in the hospital."

I wonder if Puff is a Good Citizen. I'd better put her in the basket, just in case. "Stay away from the cookie bag," I say sternly.

She meows.

SENIOR CENTER

**Kids Just Like You**
Nine-year-old Stacey found out some police departments didn't have money for bulletproof vests for their dogs. So she started Pennies to Protect Police Dogs—and bought hundreds of vests!

We're about to go inside, when I spot Anita. She smiles and waves at me.

I decide to try an ollie. Maybe I'll nail it and impress her. I take a deep breath. Pop down, snap up, and soar!

Pop. Snap—

SPLAT!

Anita rushes over. "Are you okay, Ty?"

"Fine," I mumble. But I'm embarrassed—and Mimi's giggling doesn't help.

I brush myself off and try to change the subject.

"I'm here to do a volunteer project," I explain.

"I'm visiting my grandpa," Anita tells me. We walk toward the senior center. "Oh, Ty—" she says, "about your ollies—"

Just then the door flies open, and a lady spots my basket. "Ooh, more goodies!" She pulls us inside.

**Kids Just Like You**
Nadia has been volunteering since she was eight. She sings for the people in a nursing home. She says, "Making someone happy makes you happy, and they make others happy, and it's like a chain."

Before I can stop her, she opens the lid.
*Zoom!* Puff whizzes across the room and streaks
right up the drapes. Somebody screams.

Anita charges after Puff.

"My math homework!" Mimi wails.

What a mess. My three volunteer projects have
turned into a triple-size disaster!

After everything calms down, I pick up the bag of broken cookies. "I guess nobody will want to buy these now," I say.

The lady laughs. "Probably not . . . but I think we can figure something out."

Next thing I know, I'm selling cakes and pies—and handing out free cookie samples!

Everybody is impressed by how fast I make change. It's easy, I tell them—if you're good at math, like me.

### Kids Just Like You
When their grandpa got sick, thirteen-year-old Molly and eleven-year-old Carly wanted to raise money for the American Cancer Society. They started selling honey from their family's beehives. Two years later, Hives for Lives has donated thousands of dollars!

I feel a tug on my sleeve.

Oops—I forgot about Mimi again!

"As soon as the bake sale is over, I'll help you with that homework," I promise.

"I'm already done!" she says. "Anita's grandpa helped me. He used to be a math teacher!"

When the bake sale ends, I find Anita. "Thanks
for getting Puff down from the drapes," I tell her.

"No problem," she says. "You helped me, too.
Now I know what to do for *my* volunteer project."

"What?" I ask. "Tutoring? Pet-sitting?"

"Come to the park tomorrow and you'll see,"
she tells me. "And Ty—bring your skateboard."

Anita's project is awesome! With her help, I'm doing perfect ollies in no time. I even volunteer to help the other kids.

"Pop down, snap up, and soar," I tell Nate. "Simple!" It takes a little practice, but he gets it.

ANITA'S
SKATEBOARD
CLINIC—FREE

Even Mimi is catching on. She's popping a mini-ollie!

Volunteering is really pretty cool!

Now, if I could only learn to do a casper or a kickflip. . . .

### Make It a Team Sport
Think about volunteering with a friend—or even with your whole family! One person can make a big difference, but lots of people can make a **bigger** difference!

*I can work with others!*

# MAKING CONNECTIONS

Have you ever heard someone say, "Two heads are better than one?" It doesn't mean you should try to grow an extra head. It means that working with others can help you come up with ideas you might never have thought of on your own!

## Look Back
- On page 13, what does Mr. Soo tell Ty? On the next page, how does Ty come up with his idea to tutor Mimi?
- Look at pages 26–27. What happens to the cookies? How does Ty get involved in the bake sale?
- On page 29, how do you think Anita came up with the idea for her volunteer project? (Hint: Look at pages 22–23.)

## Try This!
Volunteering is a great way to show off the things you're good at—and help other people at the same time! There are lots of ways to be a volunteer. Get started by making a list of your skills.

• Are you good at math or science? How about helping younger kids with their homework? • Do you like baking? You could bake cookies to donate to a good cause. • Is there a sport you're especially good at? You might help someone improve their skills.

Check out senior centers in your community. Get together with friends, and volunteer. Remember, anything you know can be shared with others. Just give it a try!